D

 Suffolk County Council

Libraries & Heritage

White Wolves Series Consultant: Sue Ellis,
Centre for Literacy in Primary Education

This book can be used in the White Wolves Guided Reading programme
with children who need a lot of support with reading at Year 4 level

First published 2007 by
A & C Black Publishers Ltd
38 Soho Square, London, W1D 3HB

www.acblack.com

Text copyright © 2007 James Riordan
Illustrations copyright © 2007 Matilda Harrison

ISBN 978-0-7136-8213-7

A CIP catalogue for this book is available from the British Library.

This book is produced using paper that is made from wood grown
in managed, sustainable forests. It is natural, renewable and
recyclable. The logging and manufacturing processes conform
to the environmental regulations of the country of origin.

Printed and bound in Great Britain by MPG Books Limited.

The Little Puppet Boy

James Riordan

Illustrated by Matilda Harrison

A & C Black • London

Contents

Chapter One

In a lonely cottage, deep in the
forest, an old woman was sitting
with her grandaughter, Lenochka.
Giant fir trees were

waving their
arms wildly
in the
snowstorm,
casting
shadows
on the

walls. From the trees came the howling of wolves.

"I'm scared," said Lenochka. "If only I had a doll to protect me."

Granny smiled. She fetched her basket of odds and ends, saying, "Mmmm. Straw sack for body, arms and legs. Red cloak, blue trousers. Wooden head, and old mop for hair."

"What about eyes and mouth?" asked the girl.

"Let's see. Blue buttons for eyes, painted red lips and a carrot for a nose. How's that?"

What a funny little fellow he was!

"What are we going to call him?" asked Granny.

"Petroushka," said Lenochka at once.

Just then, a tinkling bell was heard. It was Grandad returning on his sleigh. Lenochka's mother was sick and he had been to visit her in hospital.

Grandad sat down and ate some soup, before speaking.

"She's asking for Lenochka," he said at last.

"Then you must take the girl to see her mother," his wife replied.

Early the next day, Grandad prepared his horse, and Lenochka eagerly took her seat in the sleigh. Petroushka sat beside her, a happy grin on his face.

"Gee-up!" cried Grandad and the horse set off, trotting down the snowy track.

They hadn't gone far when
they heard the howling of wolves.

Wooo-oo-oooo! Wooo-oo-oooo!

The howling came closer and
closer. Now and then, they saw
grey shadows in the forest.

All at once, a pack of hungry
wolves broke from the trees and
ran behind the sleigh.

The leader came so close that Lenochka could feel its hot breath. At any moment it was going to drag her to the ground.

Then, all of a sudden, a very strange thing happened.

Petroushka flew from the little girl's side and hit the leader on the head. The rest of the pack skidded to a halt, thinking he was food.

While the wolves were tearing at the rag doll, Grandad drove the horse on and they made their escape. It wasn't long before they reached their destination.

Lenochka's mother was astonished to hear her daughter's story.

"Petroushka saved your life," she said.

"And now you've lost him. Never mind. I feel much better, so I'm coming to look after you now."

The little girl clapped her
hands with joy and, later that day,
all three set off in the sleigh on
their return. Along the way, they
passed some hunters.

"Watch out for wolves," called
Grandad. He told them of their
narrow escape.

The sleigh rushed on and the hunters continued along the path. All of a sudden, they stopped.

What was that?

A face was grinning up at them! It belonged to a bundle of rags propped up against a fir tree.

"Looks like he's been in the wars, poor fellow," said one. "I'll take him home to my wife. She'll soon patch him up."

And so Petroushka found himself being washed, stitched and filled with fresh straw. This time he was given a cherry-red nose and an old checked cap; then the woman painted freckles on his cheeks. He looked funnier than ever.

19

Since she had no children of
her own, the hunter's wife gave the
doll to a shop in town. A sign was
stuck on him:

Petroushka
The Clown
One Rouble

This was just the start of
Petroushka's adventures.

Chapter Two

One day, a puppet master saw
the rag doll in the window and
bought him.

"You can be
the clown in
my show, lad.
With your
big grin and
funny face,
the children
will love you."

After several months' travelling from town to town, the puppet show came to St Petersburg. It was the Easter Fair and the showground was crowded.

Soldiers walked by, all spick and span, raising their hats to passing girls. A red-faced sergeant proudly twisted his long moustache.

Shrieking children played hide and seek, in and out of the pie stalls. They begged their mothers for a ride on the swings or merry-go-round. Painted horses spun above their heads.

On every side, stalls were bright with toys, coloured balloons and goldfish in glass bowls. Clouds of steam rose above the crowds, slowly fading in the frosty air. All about was hustle and bustle.

Suddenly, there was a drum roll.

"Ladies and Gentlemen,"
shouted an officer in plum-red
uniform. "Listen to the band."

The sound of music
filled the fair.

"Roll up! Roll up!" a jolly man was shouting. "All the fun of the fair. Come and see the greatest show on earth. See Strongman thrill you with his daring feats of strength."

It was the puppet master who had bought Petroushka for a rouble.

"See Pretty Ballerina," he cried. "Her dancing will take your breath away.

"See Old Bones the Skeleton. He'll send chills up and down your spine."

Puffing out his cheeks, the puppet master shouted, "And your very own ... the ever popular ... Petroushka the Clown."

While the man was introducing the show, a mother and child were pushing through the crowd. The girl's cheeks were red from frost and she was tugging at her mother's hand.

"Come on, Mama," she cried. "Hurry up. I want to see little Petroushka."

"Of course," her mother said. "How can we come to the fair without seeing the clown?"

Soon they were standing at the very front of the stage, staring up at the little theatre.

Suddenly, the red velvet
curtains parted to reveal golden
sands. Beside a cactus in a desert
stood the giant figure of
Strongman. He had a turban on
his head and a curved sword at his
belt. His white teeth sparkled
beneath a thick, black moustache.

Slowly, he raised his arms, showing off his muscles.

The crowd gasped in admiration.

Then all heads turned as Pretty Ballerina made her entry. She looked beautiful in a silver tutu and a gold taffeta skirt.

Soldiers whistled. Nursemaids blushed. Children stared wide-eyed.

Strongman caught her by the waist and swept her off in a wild dance.

At the end of the dance, the curtains closed to loud applause. When they opened again, the scene was a snowy plain. Strongman and Pretty Ballerina had gone. The stage was empty.

All at once, the mood changed and the crowd gasped in horror. Old Bones the Skeleton slowly stepped across the stage, waving his bony arms and grinning from a bare skull. His bones clinked and clanked as he hopped about, sending shivers up people's spines.

Finally, he took off his head, put it under his arm and left the stage to hisses and boos.

For a few moments, there was silence. Then a small figure appeared. The funny little fellow had large eyes and a cherry-red nose. He took two steps, fell flat on his face and then looked up with a grin.

After kicking up his heels in a Russian dance, he ran into the wings.

The children laughed and cried out, "Petroushka, dear Petroushka!"

The little clown was their favourite. They did not know that beneath the grin was a broken heart.

Chapter Three

After Petroushka, the curtains closed and the puppet master shouted, "Interval. Fifteen minutes."

During the break, he went round the crowd, selling hot pies and a sticky sweet cockerel on a stick.

"All he thinks of is money," said the little girl's mother.

Still, she bought her daughter a hot pie and a sweet cockerel.

After the interval, the show started up again. As before, Strongman was standing centre stage. Sword raised, he was staring at the crowd, as if daring anyone to fight him.

The women and children drew
back in fear; even the soldiers
seemed scared of his fierce look.

When no one took up the
challenge, Strongman put the
sword back into his belt and
glanced to one side.

Pretty Ballerina made her
entry in a gold and silver costume.
No sooner had she appeared
than Strongman seized her
roughly by the waist, threw her

up into the air and caught her
as she fell. Then, as the music
played, he whirled her round and
round so fast, the two became
a blur.

As they were dancing, the little
clown looked on in the
wings. From the
crowd, the little
girl noticed him
and saw the love
in his eyes for
Pretty Ballerina.

"How sad
Petroushka looks,"
she murmured.

39

Pretty Ballerina heard her. "Poor Petroushka," she thought. "He loves me dearly and does all he can to please me. No one else cares. Not the cruel Strongman. Not the mean old puppet master. Certainly not the heartless skeleton – he has no feelings for anybody. They all think only of themselves."

Just then, Strongman tossed Pretty Ballerina into the air again, taking her breath away – and she forgot all about Petroushka in the heat of the dance.

But Petroushka did not forget her. That night, after the show, he lay in his dark box, all alone. Two big tears rolled down his cheeks.

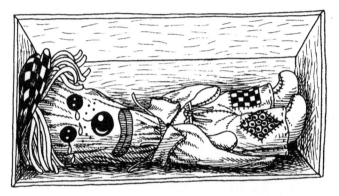

"I'm tired of being a clown," he sniffed. "Oh, Pretty Ballerina, if only I were big and brave, I would save you from Strongman. I would take you in my arms and fly far, far away."

He sighed.

"But I'm only a rag doll, a clown who makes people laugh. Pretty Ballerina is too beautiful to take any notice of me."

He sighed again.

"No, there's nothing to be done. I'm too weak and not brave at all."

Then a thought came to him. He remembered Lenochka and the hungry wolves.

"Wait a minute! Who was it that saved the little girl from the wolves? If I was brave enough to do that, I can stand up to Strongman."

He had made up his mind and there, in the darkness of his box, he took a vow.

"Tomorrow I shall challenge Strongman to a duel. Then Pretty Ballerina will see how brave I am."

Chapter Four

Next day, a crowd gathered before
the puppet theatre once more. The
little girl and her mother were at
the front again. As usual, the show
opened with the desert dance.

Strongman and Pretty
Ballerina began leaping about the
stage, unaware that something
unexpected was about to happen.

In the wings,
a figure stood,
watching. It was
Petroushka, pale
and determined.
With a mighty
effort, he had
pushed open the
lid of his box and
was now staring at
the stage, waiting
for his chance.

Suddenly, he heard a noise.

It was Old Bones the Skeleton creeping up behind him. He had a toothy grin on his face.

"Just look at them," hissed Old Bones. "See how closely he holds her. See how scared she is of him. How she wishes she could escape from his clutches."

The evil skeleton was doing all he could to start a fight.

"Why don't you save her?" said Old Bones.

That was all Petroushka
needed. He rushed on stage and
threw himself at Strongman.
His little fists bounced off the
astonished Strongman's chest.

"Just because you're big and
strong," Petroushka cried, "you
think you can do as you please
with Pretty Ballerina. And you

think I'm nothing but a silly clown with no feelings. Well, you're wrong. I do have feelings, and I'm going to teach you a lesson."

Strongman rolled his eyes, puffed out his chest and drew his long, curved sword.

The crowd held its breath.

Pretty Ballerina threw herself between the two. But she was knocked aside by Strongman's fist.

"Run, run, Petroushka," she screamed, "or you'll be killed for sure."

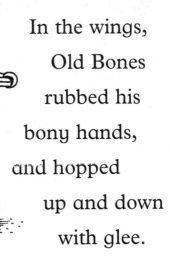

In the wings, Old Bones rubbed his bony hands, and hopped up and down with glee.

One part of the crowd looked on in horror; the other cheered, thinking this was all part of the show.

As for the puppet master, he couldn't believe his eyes.

What on earth was going on?

Then in the same breath, he muttered, "Still, why worry? As long as it brings in a crowd."

The little girl at the front cried out, "Run, Petroushka, run!"

But there was nothing that could save the little clown.

Chapter Five

Strongman stood over Petroushka, waving the sword above his head. He was shaking a fist in rage, mad that the clown had hit him.

"Run, run!" cried the children.

"Run, run!" yelled the women.

Only the men cheered, enjoying the show.

With a roar, Strongman thrust his sword deep into Petroushka's heart.

Pretty Ballerina screamed and fell down beside the lifeless clown.

For a brief moment there was silence. Then, a child's anxious voice called out, "Get up, Petroushka. Make us laugh."

But Petroushka did not move.

"It's only make believe, isn't it?" someone else asked, uncertainly.

A few moments passed and, when the rag doll didn't get up, cries went up from the crowd:

"He's dead! Strongman has killed Petroushka."

The north wind suddenly blew
through the fair, making the
grown-ups shiver and the children
cry. Why had it turned so cold?
The mother and the little girl
went to go. Their eyes were filled
with tears.

Seeing the fuss, a policeman stepped towards the puppet theatre. "What's going on here?" he asked gruffly.

"Nothing. N-n-nothing at all," the puppet master muttered. Then, pointing to Petroushka, he said, "A lot of fuss about nothing. This old rag doll needs chucking out, that's all. It's fallen to pieces."

The policeman shrugged his shoulders and, like the crowd, moved away to other stalls. If he'd stayed, he would have seen a figure on the tent top and heard a cry ring out:

"Here I am! Here I am!"

Everyone turned round.

"Look," cried the little girl. "It's Petroushka. Hooray for Petroushka!"

Others took up her cry.

"Hooray for Petroushka! Hooray, hooray, hooray!"

The puppet master's mouth fell open. He stared from the broken doll in his hand to the real, live Petroushka on the tent top, laughing happily.

Old Bones's grin faded and he shuffled off into the cold night.

Even Strongman's face turned pale.

As for Pretty Ballerina, she smiled through her tears.

The children cheered and waved their hands.

Flying high above the fair,
Petroushka danced in the frosty
sky as he'd never danced before.
Then he came down, took Pretty
Ballerina in his arms and flew
away with her across the starry
skies.

About the Author

James Riordan has written over 100 books for young people. His first novel, *Sweet Clarinet*, won the NASEN award and was shortlisted for the Whitbread Prize, and *Match of Death* won the Scottish Book Award. In his spare time, he is Visiting Professor at Worcester University.

He lives in Portsmouth, where he may be seen cycling along the seafront with his cat Tilly in a basket.

Other White Wolves from
different cultures...

The Story Thief

Andrew Fusek Peters

Nyame the sky god has a special
treasure – in a big, brass chest are
all the stories ever told. Anansi, the
cleverest of spiders, sees the people on
Earth are bored. She can't spin a tale,
but she can spin a web, so she makes a
ladder up to the sky, determined to get
back the stories, whatever it takes...

The Story Thief is a well known tale
from African folklore.

ISBN: 9 780 7136 8421 6   £4.99

Other White Wolves from
different cultures...

THE HOUND OF
ULSTER

Malachy Doyle

Little Setanta was determined
to join the Red Branch Knights,
but the king's young warriors were
determined to stop him. First he'd
have to beat them at hurling, then
he'd have to fight every one of them,
and then... then there was the great
hound of Culann to do battle with.

The Hound of Ulster is a well known
tale from Irish folklore.

ISBN: 9 780 7136 8194 9 £4.99

Year 4

Stories About Imagined Worlds

Stories That Raise Issues

Stories From Different Cultures